Magnet to the Magnate

CHARLI RAHE

TRIED AND TRUE PUBLISHING

Copyright © 2024 by Charli Rahe

All rights reserved.

No part of this book may be reproduced in any form or by any electronic or mechanical means, including information storage and retrieval systems, without written permission from the author, except for the use of brief quotations in a book review.

Cover Art by Kissable Covers

ISBN (eBook) 978-1-958055-30-4

ISBN (paperback) 978-1-958055-33-5

❦ Created with Vellum

For those of us who could use a billionaire with a marriage proposal at our front door... and my husband, who is undoubtedly disappointed that he isn't a billionaire.

Note From the Author

This story is intended for readers 18+ or those with a bit of life under their belts. With that said, please enjoy Presley and Gunner's tale.

CHAPTER 1
Gunner

"What are you watching?" My brushed leather Oxford shoes made a distinct sound over the white marble.

Torsten lifted the remote from where he sat on the kitchen stool with a chuckle. "This trial. She's a nice girl. It isn't right. All that talent. She was so good in Swan's Song."

I was a fan long before she became famous in the States. When she was modeling in Canada, I'd moved to NYC. I'd gone as far as to look into where she was in the States only to be disappointed.

"Leave it." I watched the camera pan on a familiar face framed with big, looping golden brown curls. "Presley Prince." In the court of public opinion, she was a gold digger.

The actress was dragged through the mud and back again. Slate blue eyes glossed over as her former assistant talked about her spending. It wasn't just her money, they claimed, but her ex-husband's.

Torsten pointed at the television playing on the refrigerator door. "The assistant is engaged to the husband now."

"Ex-husband," I corrected.

Barika Haik had married Presley Prince after he was a producer on her big break. Blinded By the Sun was a tragedy about the loss of a family farm in which she played the farmer's daughter. I must've watched the movie three times in the theater, only to watch it a hundred more in my theater at home. Barika was the only man she was linked to, though, according to him and Marta, the assistant, there had been several affairs. *That* I didn't believe.

Her lawyer was incompetent and Presley was going to lose more than her reputation. Barika was old money out of Egypt and had gone to Hollywood to diversify. What he really did was sleep with model after model, actress after actress. I'd bumped into him at a few events and his date was never his now ex-wife.

Presley's lack of reaction in the courtroom wasn't doing her any favors. They wanted to believe she was after him for his money and connections. As much as people fawned after beautiful people, they often wanted nothing more than to watch them crash and burn.

"She's beautiful, yes?" Torsten asked.

He turned his clear blue eyes to me. He had a severe face with flat cheekbones and red hair. Torsten was hired by my grandfather and had stayed with me after my parents died even though most of my family was back in Denmark.

"She has a team of people who make her look that way. I would know." I grinned at him and Torsten waved a hand dismissively.

"Are we headed out?" he asked as he took in my custom suit.

"The executor wants a video call." I pointed to the screen. "It will rot your brain."

Torsten waved again and smoothed his uniform tie before turning back to the screen.

Presley looked pathetically to her ex-husband as Marta left the stand.

* * *

Torsten cautiously knocked on my office door. I lifted my head and inhaled sharply before closing my laptop. "Mr. Laugesen?"

I cleared my throat. "My grandfather died."

Torsten lean frame entered my office. "Oh, Gunner. My condolences."

We weren't close, but he was my last living relative that didn't make me want to run in the opposite direction.

"Thank you, Torsten. He..." I scoffed and shook my head. "He wants to leave me everything. *Wanted*."

Torsten offered a smile. "This is great news, yes?"

I smiled incredulously and shook my head. "I have six months to get married and start having children or it all goes to Mads."

Torsten waited for the punchline.

"I'm thirty years old. I have plenty of time for that later *if* I want it. I'm not sure I do."

"Do you want the business or is it the money? You don't need it," he reminded me.

I opened my laptop up again and saw my face in the camera that was still running. My father had married the most famous model in Denmark. I'd inherited her looks and nothing from my father except his mind for business. I had coloring typical for my background; amber-blonde hair, narrow blue eyes, and I tanned well. I took care of my body so I could date any woman I wanted and did. A wife would hinder that. A child would end my life as I knew it.

"What of Melanie?" Torsten asked. "She likes you very much."

She made a great date — smart, beautiful, and well-known in my circles since she was on a number of charity boards. Melanie also had a domineering oil magnate for a father who had hinted at dating her if I planned to keep seeing her.

"We haven't spoken since that library fundraiser months ago." I sighed. "You can retire for the day. Ask Olga if a late lunch will work. I'm going to do some work while I think."

Torsten bobbed his head. "I am sorry about your grandfather. I will let Olga know."

"Thank you, Torsten."

Instead of working, I decided that what I really needed was a distraction. Since Torsten found it so entertaining, I decided to search the trial every couch potato with no life was watching.

Presley's look at her ex-husband with her former assistant wasn't that of a woman upset her plot didn't work. It was hurt. She'd loved him, and trusted her.

I dug a little deeper.

Presley lost a multi-movie deal based on a bestselling psychological thriller book series after Barika sued her for spending his fortune on vacations with supposed lovers, of which there was no photographic evidence of and gifts for the invisible lovers of which the only receipts are on credit cards in both their names. As flimsy as the case was, the production companies weren't taking any chances with one of their biggest backers. They cut ties with Presley and she was blacklisted. After the trial, she'd likely owe her ex-husband for his affair. I had no doubt that he was the one doing exactly what he accused her of and had been plotting her public humiliation for some time. She never saw it coming, that much was clear.

An hour or so into my online stalking, my phone vibrated across the desk. I checked the name and my mood soured.

"How are you, Mads?" I answered.

"Saddened by the death of farfar. Aren't you?"

"Of course. You're sure you're not calling to see if he left me anything?"

"You were his favorite. I assume he left you everything he could get away with without imploding our family. I did get a few properties here and in Gothenburg and Bergen."

Farfar had spent a massive fortune of his two primary residences. I doubted Mads had to marry to get them.

"That's it then? The estates?"

"A villa in Sicily not worth mentioning. It's too hot there. Though, the women are beautiful. You remember."

I inhaled and ran my hand over my mouth. "Is anyone arranging services? A memorial or something?"

"Nej. He wanted nothing. They're sliding his body out into the arctic circle where he'll likely be eaten by polar bears or killer whales."

"It was lovely to hear from you, Mads. Try not to drop dead too soon."

"You as well. At least not before I meet your wife." He hung up in a bout of laughter.

I could've wallowed, but I knew exactly what would cheer me up.

I scrolled to Melanie's name and dialed.

* * *

Sleeping was a luxury I never had a problem indulging in until some crotchety executor callously told me about my grandfather's death and followed-up with a ticking time bomb.

Olga smiled at me as I entered the kitchen. She had a streak of grey in her long brunette hair that she tied into a chignon.

Torsten poured me a mug of coffee and smiled, too. "Good morning."

"You look bad, Gunner," Olga lectured. "Did you sleep?"

"Not a wink." I groaned as I sat and nodded to Torsten. "Thank you." I sipped. "I fell asleep about ten minutes before my alarm went off."

"Is that because Miss Kelley was here?" Olga pried.

Melanie was easy to talk to, and even easier not to talk to. There was something holding me back from actually liking her. I didn't mind her and she looked damn good in my bed.

"I'm afraid there was no marriage proposal," I joked.

Olga looked up from where she cooked my breakfast and smirked. "Good. Everything has been handed to her. She would fall apart if anything happened that her assistant didn't warn her of."

That was true.

"She's a nice young woman," Torsten argued.

"I didn't say she wasn't nice. I said she was weak-minded." Olga pointed her wooden spoon covered in egg whites at him. "No one is speaking to you."

Torsten smiled at his wife and looked back to the tablet he read the news on every morning.

My eyes slid to the screen. Presley Prince had to pay her insanely wealthy husband for dissipation and it would cost her everything she owned. I knew because I looked up her worth. Her career was over at twenty-eight when it was just getting good.

"That poor girl." Olga brought three plates to the counter of the sprawling marble kitchen.

I'd intended on adding color eventually, but the decorator said high contrast black and white was in at the time I purchased it.

"She looked shocked," Torsten agreed.

"Pretty girl like her? She'll be alright." I accepted Olga's plate of egg whites, mushrooms, and spinach. "Thank you."

Olga kissed the top of my head. She was barely old enough

to be mistaken for my mother, but my mother never had her warmth. "You're welcome. Do you want to watch Swan's Song tonight? You love that movie."

My favorite Presley Prince movie would've been depressing if her portrayal of the teenage singer that tragically dies after her first big performance wasn't some of the best acting I'd ever witnessed. I didn't think it was bias. She was talented.

"I'd like that."

CHAPTER 2
Presley

I thanked the driver and quickly exited the vehicle. He recognized me and if I had one more stranger tell me I was a horrible person I was going to start believing them. I was stupid, not evil. I believed Barika when he told me he was traveling for work until Marta confronted me and said she was quitting to be with him. I'd had no idea. She lived with us. Our entire marriage was a lie.

I stood outside of the last place I owned — the first purchase I made with my big break paycheck that didn't have Barika's name on it. My sad little SoHo apartment was more than I could afford and when I sold it, that money would go to Barika, too.

"Miss Prince?"

I cringed and turned to the person on the sidewalk looking at me. My pasted-on smile wasn't fooling anyone.

"Yes?"

"This is a Notice to Appear."

She handed me a manilla envelope and I looked at it.

"He won —"

"It's for deportation proceedings. Have a great day."

She turned around.

"But... I'm getting my citizenship!" I called after her.

She didn't respond and my shoulders sagged.

My attorney gave me the list of worst-case scenarios; Barika wins and he gets everything I've ever owned or I get deported. He didn't say it could be both.

I tried to hurry inside so I could cry without a dozen photographers catching it.

A hand caught the door to the building as I swung it open and I murmured an apology.

"Miss Prince?"

"What! For the love of god, what more do I have to give!" I cried out.

So much for avoiding public humiliation.

The gorgeous man confronting me arched a straight brow. He had to be an actor. He had incredible cheekbones and a great jawline. His wavy hair furled just so and his eyes sizzled. I'd been propositioned by too many men with the same look to count. Normally, it had no effect on me. It was hardly a normal day.

"I'm Gunner Laugesen of Laugesen Shipping. I have a proposition for you if we could speak somewhere privately." He nodded his blonde head towards the door. Only his hair had a strawberry tinge to it in the sunlight.

"I don't know you." I scoffed. "What do I have to do with shipping?"

He pressed full lips together with barely masked irritation. "A lot, if you agree to marry me."

I narrowed my eyes.

"This isn't a scam." Gunner, if that was his real name, ducked his head and took out his phone. He held up a picture of himself beside an article outlining the death of his billionaire grandfather a month earlier. "I am who I say I am."

I shifted and looked down the sidewalk. Other than an

enthusiastic looking middle-aged man at the blacked-out SUV, no one was paying attention to us.

"I'm sorry. Did you say marry you?"

"In private?" He pressed and I sighed.

I was keenly aware of him behind me as we went inside the building. It had a fresh scent as if someone had lit a citronella candle in the stairway. My apartment was on the third floor and there was no elevator.

"I haven't been here this year," I muttered.

"I don't mind."

Someone had stopped by to freshen it up for me. It was an expense I allowed because I wouldn't do it myself. I barely showered. Dusting my apartment after a coast-to-coast flight wasn't happening.

It was simple with a lot of natural light and unfinished wood. I'd gone through a phase when I had my role as a farmer's daughter in the movie Barika discovered me.

I set my keys down on the handmade table. "I can offer you water, Mr. Laugesen."

"No, thank you."

He was looking at me too intently. I pulled my sorry excuse for a disguise off of my head. And threw the White Sox baseball cap beside my keys before shaking out my hair.

"I literally have no idea why you're here."

Gunner inspected the apartment in between staring at me. "I'm in a peculiar position. Currently, you are blacklisted and going to have to file bankruptcy if something doesn't change quick."

"I'm also going to get deported." I threw the envelope on the table and he stopped it with a long finger.

"Which makes your reason to accept even better."

"Accept what? That insane marriage proposal?" I demanded. "I may be having a run of bad luck —"

"I'm offering ten million," he interrupted, and I narrowed my eyes.

"Dollars?"

"Not pesos."

"For marriage?" I clarified.

His lips pressed. "I also need a child within the next few months... a pregnancy, I mean."

I grinned as I scanned his stupidly handsome face and burst out laughing. "I can't remember the last time I laughed."

"I don't appreciate you laughing in my face at my more than generous offer."

I grunted as my laughter stopped cold. "You're serious? I don't understand. You don't know me."

"I have these boxes to tick. My inheritance is contingent on it. After a year or so, you can take the money and we'll divorce."

I folded my arms and eyed him. "And this hypothetical child?"

His chest swelled with a deep inhale. "I want it." He gently cleared his throat. "You could have rights if that is what you're worried about. We can't put that in writing for now."

"Why not marry a girlfriend or someone you know?"

"Because I don't want a marriage, just a wife. This is a business transaction. However, my grandfather —"

"Your grandfather is making a grown man get married against his will?"

Gunner finally smiled.

It was quite the smile.

"He had an odd sense of humor. I'm sure he worried about me being alone or continuing our family legacy. Perhaps he was still angry with me for not going back to Denmark after my father died. He's gone and I don't know."

"I'm sorry."

He shook his head. "No one can know." He pinned me with his sharp blue eyes. "If anyone discovers the arrangement isn't real, I stand to lose everything. I will be completely cut off."

"Why do I feel like you're about to say something I won't want to hear?"

"That means we could have to look legitimate and we couldn't use a facility to aid in conception."

My lips popped open. "You're going to pay me ten million —"

"Fifteen," he countered.

"To sleep with you until I get pregnant? Wreck my body, what chance I have of a career in doing so, and give you a child?" I scoffed. "Two hundred million or it isn't worth my effort."

His eyes slid over my face and I felt my face heat as he masked the way his eyes slid over my breasts in the tank top I wore.

"Done, but you have to remain faithful. Any indiscretions will jeopardize what we're trying to do."

My temper heated. "And you?"

He inclined his head. "I don't know who my grandfather has watching us. I can't risk it. Besides, for two hundred million, I hope I don't have cause to look elsewhere."

"Funny." I gave him a flat look. "So, are you going to give me a ring or something?"

The corner of his mouth kicked up and it was my new favorite expression. He pulled a box out of his pocket and opened it. "This is yours to keep as well. To convey just how serious I am about the arrangement. It's worth more than this building."

"This is insane." I whispered as I looked at the blue rectangular cut diamond ring.

"It's the Oppenheimer Blue. I wouldn't buy just any diamond for a woman I was going to marry." He pulled the ring out and set the box aside. "Besides, it matches your eyes." He didn't catch my gaping expression as he slid the ring on my finger.

"Why me? You could have anyone."

"My driver and his wife adore you. They're hoping you land on your feet and I have the ability to help you in that. In turn, they're happy, they'll love the child we have, and I'll keep my business. Everyone wins."

"That's a good enough reason for you to marry someone?" I asked.

"No. But it's good enough for my current purposes." He met my eyes. "Are you agreeing? We'll have to move you from here and handle your legal issues straightaway. I can't have any involvement in that."

"This is crazy," I whispered.

But then, what were my alternatives?

I'd rather live on the streets than watch my mother gloat at my misfortunes.

"And I'd like to start trying to conceive right away."

"What is happening," I whispered.

"Do you track your cycle? I can download whatever application you use to track your fertility. Assuming you are fertile, that changes things."

I pressed my fingertips to my eyelids. "I'm having an out of body experience."

"Just say yes. It is that simple. We'll move you into my home in Connecticut and you can sell this place to finish settling your debt to your ex-husband. I'll take care of you for at least the next year."

"Okay," I whispered and nodded. "You've got me. I'm desperate." I shrugged. "Anything else?"

He shook his head. "There won't be a prenup so it will be on your honor that you won't take more than what I'm offering."

I nodded. "Despite all the evidence to the contrary, I typically have decent morals. I'm not a gold digger." No matter what the media claimed.

He nodded. Gunner digested my acceptance in exactly .08 seconds before he removed his designer suit jacket.

"Oh. I guess this is happening right now." I grunted again and looked around. What for? I didn't know.

I grabbed the hem of my tank top and pulled it over my head. Gunner slid his eyes over my chest as he unbuttoned his shirt.

"Any hereditary illnesses I need to know about?" he asked.

I pursed my lips. "Heart disease."

He nodded. "Mine, too."

"It's how my dad died."

He left his shirt open, displaying row upon row of carved tan muscle. "Mine as well."

"Should we kiss or something?" I asked nervously. "You're not just saying all this to sleep with me, right? That would be insane."

"I'm not." He met my eyes and something changed in his face. Gunner raised his hand and crooked his finger. "Come here."

My mouth had suddenly gone dry. I shifted my feet to use the toe of my shoe to help me out of my sneakers and shoved down my yoga pants. I managed to step out of them and not fall face first into him.

We stood so close that if either of us swayed we'd touch one another.

"You have a beautiful body," Gunner murmured and raised his hand. He took a lock of my hair and rubbed it between his fingers. "Anything off the table?"

My brows knit. "Sex wise?"

He nodded once and dropped my hair to unbuckle his belt.

I shook my head. "Just don't choke me or hurt me."

He nodded again. "What about fucking you?"

It took an effort to finish the swallow I started with my throat being so dry. "I think that's okay."

"Anal?"

I shrugged a shoulder. "That doesn't make babies."

The corner of his lips tugged up in that cute expression again. "It doesn't have to be all business. Just as long as a baby comes from it, but I also don't want you to feel obligated once you're with child."

I nodded. "I won't."

He inhaled deeply and stepped back. Gunner folded his pants and set them on the table. With his back to me, he removed his socks and boxer briefs. I took advantage of not having his eyes on me for a moment and shed my underwear and bra.

Gunner turned and I felt a pulse at his nude, muscled body. He seemed to like me, too. *Like*, a lot. Almost too much.

My stomach dropped and he stilled. "What's wrong?"

I covered my breasts with an arm. "I'm actually on my period. I'm sorry. I spaced."

"A tampon?" he asked, and my face flushed.

"Yeah." I edged for my discarded underwear and he closed the distance between us. It startled me until he kissed my throat.

I hadn't been touched in seven months. Barika had slept with me just before he gave me the divorce papers after what I thought was a trial separation. Until that moment, I had no idea he was leaving me for good.

"Are you okay?" he panted.

"Yeah."

Gunner stopped and looked down at me. "You're not."

I swallowed as he waited for an answer with his hands on my waist. "I... the last time..."

"With your ex."

I nodded. "It was just a while ago and it sucked."

His lips curled. "This won't suck."

I was going to have to take his word for it.

"Relax." He coaxed and his hand drifted along my hip to my thigh. He reversed me to the table and kissed along my shoulder.

I moaned when his fingers slid between my legs.

"Ready?"

No.

He curled a finger along the string and I felt it pull from me as he slowly removed it. I didn't know what he did with it, but I wasn't asking. He lifted my behind to the edge and fit between my legs before slanting his mouth over mine.

His hands roamed all over me. I hadn't been so thoroughly felt up in ages. His hips curled and teased just outside of me before he shifted closer.

Gunner moaned against my lips and I gasped when he began to move. It was slippery and quick. I was at a delicious angle with my heels at the small of his back and my palms bracing my weight on the table.

Gunner cursed under his breath and slowed down. I was grateful because I was going to come quick and it would be embarrassing.

"What do you like? I want it to feel good for you." He trailed kisses back to my neck, and I clenched around him. "You like that, don't you?" he breathed.

I couldn't tell him that it was his desire to please me more than the motion that got me going. I took his face and turned it to me so I could kiss him deeper.

CHAPTER 3
Gunner

Presley sat beside me in the SUV, letting me stroke my finger between her legs with no promise of anything more. Once hadn't been enough. I couldn't fuck her again with Torsten badgering her with questions she politely answered while red faced because of how I touched her.

I only made informed decisions and Presley was perfect for my needs.

She was also more down to earth than I thought she would be. Money alone wouldn't have secured her, but safety from deportation would.

"I'm sorry, Torsten." I hit the privacy screen button and it slid up between us.

Presley arched a shapely brow at me as she wryly pursed her lips. "Need something?"

I nodded with a deep inhale. "I would really enjoy it if you sucked my dick."

She glanced away, but not before her face turned red. It was a beautiful face. When she blushed I grew hard. I didn't think she was remotely shy, only surprised at how her day was shaping out and all the delicious twists and turns.

She slipped off the seatbelt. That wasn't very safe.

"On second thought, we should wait." I barely got the words out as I thought about how close I was to getting her mouth around my dick.

"Want me to wear the seatbelt?" she teased and I almost groaned aloud.

"Please." I inclined my head and she buckled again.

Presley leaned over and unzipped my fly. Her face was inches away from mine.

"You've got a nice dick, Gunner. I'm surprised you know how to use it."

What did *that* mean?

Before I could voice the question, she ducked down and thoughts evaporated. There was only Presley's mouth sliding up and down my dick.

Once again, it was over in minutes. She came in the apartment, but I was going to have to make up the blow job to her.

She straightened and I licked the corner of my mouth as she brushed hers with the side of her hand. "What's the verdict?"

"Letter grade or praise?" I asked suppressing a smirk.

I could've framed the saucy grin she shown my way. "Well, damn. Since you're getting specific give me both."

I lifted my hips and tucked myself away. "Denmark has a point-based scale. You're a twelve with no room for improvement and give a world class blow job."

She barked a laugh and turned away while shaking her head. "A+?"

"As high as it goes."

"It sure does." Her head slid back to me. "Barika made me take a class." I shifted to look at her. "Is that crass for me to mention?"

I shook my head. "It was crass of him to demand unless you wanted to."

She glanced away again. "I didn't. Thank you for being kind."

"That wasn't generosity. I have no motivation to lie. On the contrary."

She nodded absently as she stared through the tinted window. "That's fair."

"Tell me more about yourself," I asked to diffuse the tension but it sprung up thicker.

"My dad was the one who raised me until he had a heart attack at forty-five. I was eight — just old enough to know my mom shouldn't be alone with me. She gambled every penny he made, but he loved her so much." She inhaled and flashed me a fake smile. "She took everything I made modeling as a child until I was sixteen and ran away. I was lucky. I stayed with friends, she only ever got in touch for money. I made it to the States with a boyfriend way too old for me, auditioned for everything I could find, finally got gigs, and he did the same thing. It wasn't until I left NYC for LA that my life became what I envisioned." She scoffed. "But really it was another person manipulating me into thinking I had control. Barika found me fresh off my success. Everyone I used — agents, lawyers, accountants — all of it, they were his. So, when he left me... The story gets old fast. I won't take all your money when we divorce, but I am going to make sure I don't get fucked over again, Gunner."

I reached for her face and she watched me with narrowed eyes. "I have an obscene amount of money and regardless of how this pans out, you *will* have my child and I want you looked after."

She wanted to believe me. It was written all over her face.

I leaned forward and she waited as I kissed her before kissing me back.

"You must be very good at what you do," she whispered against my lips.

CHARLI RAHE

"I am."

CHAPTER 4

Presley

The rest of the car ride to his estate was spent discussing finances and details of our arrangement. Gunner spent a lot of time on the phone with his attorney, who was not in on our plots.

There'd be no big ceremony. We'd quietly get married, I'd get the first payment immediately afterwards, and Gunner wanted to start the process for dual citizenship right away. He also suggested suing Barika for emotional distress, but I wanted that chapter of my life closed.

Gunner wasn't humble and was often blunt. After years of sugarcoating or straight-up lying to my face, it felt confrontational. He wasn't quite New York and he wasn't LA. Maybe he was common for Danes.

Gunner rolled down the privacy screen so Torsten's beaming face was back in the rearview mirror. No one had to tell me that the lines were blurred between them as he began to pepper me with more questions about the movies I'd been in.

* * *

Gunner listened with an amused smile as he was on his phone. I hoped he was smiling over our interaction and not whatever woman he was undoubtedly snubbing with our arrangement. There would be at least one, possibly dozens. As soon as I had a free moment, I was going to research the shit out of him.

"Welcome to Birdsong Estate, Miss Prince." Torsten's endless enthusiasm was infectious.

I was used to mansions along the west coast. Gunner's home was more like Barika's unscrupulous friends in Europe. Black art nouveau gates opened with a scrolling "L" at its center. It was pure white stone with a black tiled roof and arching windows along its three floors. Without having to enter, I knew the interior would be similar. Something classic with high contrast colors, and sprawling. The money he must've invested into it was daunting.

"It is ironically named for the Danish national bird — the mute swan," Torsten excitedly explained, and met my eyes in the rearview mirror.

Suddenly, things made sense.

"Like, the ugly duckling," I noted with a coy smirk.

It was my big break movie; a high school adaptation where I was an outcast but my shining personality, and a hefty makeover, showed through and quieted the upperclassman bullies with an emotional concert in which I sang. At the end, my character was hit by a car while closing her eyes, savoring the applause and acceptance of my classmates. I had been twenty-three playing a sixteen-year-old and won a Golden Globe, Critic's Choice, and People's Choice awards for the role.

Impossibly, Torsten grew more animated. "Yes! Like, your movie. Gunner's mother —"

"We watched that movie in the theater," Gunner interrupted.

Torsten quieted down and cast sympathetic looks at Gunner. I'd have to ask him about it later.

Torsten stopped on the white pavers that made up the winding driveway and hurried around the SUV to open my door. Gunner opened his own and waited.

All my belongings had already been in boxes so it was easy to make the switch from the apartment to the car. What I left would be brought later or sold, including the apartment. Gunner's attorney already set it in motion with the realtor he used.

I still couldn't tell if I had lucked out or if I was continuing a dangerous path of stupidity.

Gunner held out his hand to me and Torsten poorly hid a smile before I accepted.

"For the time being, it's prudent we share a room." Gunner's statement didn't distract me from the trek up the sweeping stone steps to the scrollwork double doors of his estate.

"Prudent, is it?" I mused.

Gunner stopped us in the three-story foyer. As suspected, he came from Barika's kind of money. The kind Hollywood catered to for funding. The décor was art, each piece curated, and done in black and white. Not a color to be found. It was a museum and in desperate need of warmth.

"You can have your own room."

"Gunner?" A woman called. "Did you see her? Are you going to see her? Oh." A lovely woman a little too young to be my mom's age blushed and wiped her hands along the front of an apron tied around her waist. "Gunner, you should've called ahead." She smoothed invisible locks into a chignon.

"I thought Torsten would. Olga, this is Presley. I invited her to live here and hide out from the press. This is Torsten's wife — she does the cooking and cleaning so if there's something specific you'd like she is who you'd tell."

Torsten entered behind us and stepped beside Olga with one of my boxes. "She's even more beautiful in person."

I got that a lot and it no longer made me blush. "Thank you."

Olga fanned herself. "When his farfar —"

"It was a long drive, Olga. Maybe something light while we freshen up?" Gunner took my hand again.

Olga nodded with a smile. "I'm so glad you accepted. This place is private. Gunner owns the lands all around it. No paparazzi will find you or your awful ex-husband. Our Gunner —"

"Excuse us, Olga." Gunner cut to the left to one of the sweeping stairways to the second floor.

He pulled me into the furthest room at the end of the hall glowing with natural lighting.

I opened my mouth to gape at the room and its ceiling high white tufted headboard under a giant chandelier. It was obscenely decadent.

Gunner took advantage of my distraction and lifted me up by my thighs. I gasped and fell forward into him where his mouth was strategically ready.

I moaned as he carried me to the bed and laid over me.

Gunner was going to break my heart and I didn't know how to stop it.

CHAPTER 5
Gunner

I rubbed my thumb along my fist as I watched Presley swim in the outdoor pool. It was a beautiful morning and I wanted nothing more than to join her — my wife. The fine hair on my arm stood-on end and I rolled up my sleeve to see it. Three months and my dick still got hard looking at her.

She didn't look like she was entering her second trimester. Presley looked gorgeous anytime of the day. I romanticized her. I knew that. She wasn't a clear image in my mind, only feelings. Other than the announcement of our marriage and then her pregnancy, we remained quiet against the barrage of reporters trying to get any tidbit from us. I expected it and employed my own people to stop them, including security to protect the property and accompany Presley if she left the estate. She didn't.

The fact that Presley lived her everyday life under the microscope, with strangers shredding anything she did, made me sad for her. She deserved better and I would make sure she'd have it.

Olga stepped beside me and held the side of my head so

she could bring it to her lips as she reached on her tiptoes. She kissed my temple and squeezed my arm before leaning into me. Presley had won her over long before she arrived and that feeling had only intensified for both Olga and Torsten.

"She is perfect, Gunner. She is the one for you."

I smirked. "I should hope so since you witnessed our wedding and had your ear to the door when the doctor confirmed that she's carrying my child."

Never in my life had I been with a woman the way I had been with Presley immediately following the doctor's departure. I wanted to impregnate all over again, to fill her up. I wanted to watch the rosy glow spread across her cheeks and linger on her chest when she met my eyes.

How hard my dick was got awkward with Olga standing beside me.

"All you needed was a push from your farfar. The right woman," she waved her hands, "appeared."

"Olga, I drove hours to get to her doorstep and all but begged her to give me a chance."

She smiled up at me and pinched my cheek. She only did that when she was feeling nostalgic. Olga and Torsten had been looking after me for as long as I could remember.

We watched Presley get out of the pool. There was a slight roundness to her stomach and her breasts swelled against the indigo bikini.

"It's a beautiful day for a swim."

A smile curled my lips as I continued to watch Presley. "Is that you dropping hints?"

"These days go too quick. Best enjoy them."

Presley laid on the white lounger and stretched out. She leaned and pulled off her top.

Olga giggled. "Torsten is going to faint."

I chuckled and stepped from the window.

I didn't bother with a pitstop to my room. There was no way I was wearing anything once I reached the pool.

I stepped out onto the stretch before the pool and saw a man standing beside a topless Presley. She wasn't even bothering to cover herself. The man wore a navy suit with pale blonde hair that brushed the collar. I stormed over to Presley as the man turned.

Mads grinned brightly at me with sly blue eyes. "How are you, cousin?" He looked back at Presley who was finally putting her top back on. "I met your wife. I was disappointed not to get an invite." He shielded his eyes when he looked to me again.

"Go put something on," I growled at Presley.

She blinked at me before reaching for the towel on the table beside her.

"Excuse me," she whispered as she passed beside us while I stared Mads down.

He purposely checked her out.

"That was rude."

I stepped closer to Mads. "Take your eyes off my wife."

Mads kept my eye contact. "We had bets on whether or not you were paying her to put up with you. I'm proud of you, Gunner. Presley Prince? She changed her name — Presley Laugesen. "

I drew in a long easing breath. "We find out what we're having in a few weeks."

Mads clapped a hand on my shoulder. "Congratulations. I'll pray for a son."

"I'll tell her to come down. Olga can get lunch ready."

Mads let his hand drop. "I'll see you there."

I hurried back into the house and jogged up the stairs. Presley turned to see who was behind her and staggered back when I didn't slow. She gasped as I kissed her and spun her around. She freed her arm and drew back to slap me. My cheek stung and I glared at her. She kept my eyes and slowly turned around so she faced the back windows that overlooked the pool.

We could see Mads on a call looking into the water. Presley's thumbs hooked in her briefs and she drew them down just under her cheeks. Her back bowed and I took sure steps to her. My tie lassoed around her wrists and I pulled her top up over her breasts.

Her ass ground on me. I yanked my zipper down and parted through my pants. My only thought was to be inside of her.

First on the balcony and then on all fours. I stretched her arms as I kept her pinned under me. We had rug burns from it.

We didn't speak in the rush to get our clothes back on and down to Mads. Olga was already mixing a meal up and Torsten handled the drinks. Afterwards, we retired to the sitting area where there was a tiered chandelier and circular tufted couch was in a round room with a wall of windows.

Mads was staying the night. He was going to try to seduce Presley if given half a chance. His competitive streak knew no bounds. It was his greed that kept him from inheriting our family shipping company.

Presley arched a brow at me as I stood in the doorway of our shared closet. It was more of a display room, artfully lit with by incandescent sconces. She changed out of her dress and into one of the nighties I bought her. I'd splurged and filled the closet with items I thought would look good on her. She deserved to be spoiled.

Presley's smile grew as the fabric slid down her curves. "You're being awfully possessive for my fake husband."

"I'm your real husband," I reminded her and her smile deepened.

"You've got me there." She sauntered towards me knowing just how gorgeous she looked. "A lot of people saw me topless in my last movie, Gunner. People would try to catch me in-person before that so I decided to take control. I wasn't in a vulnerable position, he was, because I knew just how bad he wanted to see."

She stopped in front of me and I lifted my hand to touch her thick, silky hair. "I shouldn't have spoken to you that way." My eyes locked on hers. "You're special to me and I didn't like him invading your personal space."

Presley wound her arms around my neck. "I like you, Gunner. You spoil me, though. It's going to be hard to find anyone that comes close."

I ran my hands along her ribs to her curves and back up as I gazed down at her. "Finish getting ready for bed. I need you to do something for me."

She pulled her arms down and leaned to steal a kiss. "Sure thing."

I watched the silk of the nightie swing under her ass as she went into the bathroom.

The drawer beckoned. It smoothly slid open as if it knew I was coming. I picked up the straps that ended in cuffs and shut it.

When Presley stepped into the bedroom her brows quirked at my nudity. She reached for the thin straps of her nightie and I held up my hand.

"I'm not going to be able to sleep if I know you can get up and bump into him in the night."

Her nipples hardened visibly against the thin fabric. "You're going to have to give me a good reason to stay put."

I bit my lower lip and my dick responded with a drip of dew to the floor. "I was hoping you'd give me a reason not to worry."

Her lips parted and she inhaled shakily.

CHAPTER 6
Presley

Gunner's eyes watching me as he sat against the tufted bed, strapped to the frame so he couldn't touch me while I rode him, was hands down the sexiest thing I'd ever experienced. Mads stayed two more days, nettling Gunner and flirting relentlessly with me. Every night, Gunner gave me complete control while Mads was visiting. If he was trying to discourage me, he was failing, I sought it out when Gunner was watching. I made it up to him later.

Gunner held my hand as we left the ultrasound appointment. Two — a perfect boy and a perfect girl. I rested my head on his shoulder the entire drive and he periodically kissed it.

I'd fallen for the enigmatic, determined, beautiful shipping magnate. My shipmate through what started as a ridiculous journey to get my life back by any means necessary and help him in the process. Along the way, I fell hard. Gunner hadn't changed. He was the same man as the one I met and I didn't know what that meant for us. If I would have a place to live when the year was up.

Money could accomplish many things including getting my citizenship. We had an exclusive scheduled to try to get my career back on course, Gunner's idea, and we were attending a charity gala for children in NYC. I'd only ever gone with Barika. Gunner said he would likely be there, which I knew to be true because I'd attended the event once with him. After that, he said he needed to show off his actresses. He'd been sleeping with all of them.

Gunner warned that he would have more than a few of his walking about. I didn't know how I felt about that, especially after he said there wasn't a large gap between one of them and me. Gunner had tried to date one for a few weeks.

"You're still thinking about the woman I dated."

"Is it dated or tried to date? You're changing your story."

He chuckled and kissed the top of my head again. "I saw Swan's Song in the theater five times."

"No wonder you had such an unsuccessful dating life."

"I couldn't know you were out there alone without at least trying."

I hugged my arms around him. "That's the nicest thing anyone's ever said to me."

"I'll work hard to top it." Gunner held me back.

"Who knew the key to a happy marriage was to have a fake one?" I teased, and Gunner shifted to raise my chin to him.

"Does it still feel fake to you?"

I met his eyes. "I didn't expect this to get serious."

"My feelings are serious."

"Everything about you is serious," I wryly mused.

Gunner gently smiled. "I have to be."

"I think that's why you like me."

Gunner ran his thumb along my jaw. "You are surprisingly light for someone who plays such weighty roles."

I withdrew and took his hand in my lap. "Ah. Yes. My dreams of winning an Oscar."

"You're just getting started, Presley."

I pressed my lips together. "My birth name was Penny —

Penny Bagshaw. I changed it when I was old enough. I didn't want to be that girl anymore. I thought you should know."

"You're Presley Laugesen, my wife and soon-to-be mother. You haven't been that girl for a long time."

I shifted and rested my head on his shoulder again. "You're too sweet to me. I'm never going to leave."

"So, don't."

Heat rolled in my belly at his sweet sentiment.

"We *have* to go to the gala?" I asked curiously.

"I do. I'd like you with me, by my side, so we can put a fresh face on your public image. You deserve that Oscar, Presley. This began to help one another out and, other than giving you a place to live, I haven't held up my end of things."

I tried not to pout. "What about the Denmark trip tomorrow?"

"It'll be a vacation to see where the chips fall after our first big public outing."

People would pay for Gunner's confidence.

CHAPTER 7
Gunner

Magenta was her color. The fitted gown that emphasized her belly was absolutely stunning on Presley. I couldn't wait to show her and our happiness off. Torsten would keep the engine running in case we need to make a quick getaway.

The chances of things getting uncomfortable were strong. Melanie, as well as at least ten other women I'd seen on occasion would be at the gala as well as Barika. Marta might've been with him, but his pattern was to bring in fresh talent, as he called them.

Presley was more nervous than she was letting on. She'd gone through life that way — putting on a false outward face. I wanted her to know she could be safe — would be safe — with me.

"Tell me I look beautiful."

I chuckled as we walked up the carpeted stairs with flashes following us along with the calls of her name to get her attention.

"Were the first thirty times not enough?" I asked playfully.

"Thirty-one is my favorite number," she whispered through a smile I used to love.

It was her false smile and I despised that she had to give it to the people who had turned on her six short months ago.

"You are and always have been breathtaking." I kissed her cheek as we reached the entrance and the flashes increased.

We took steps inside and she squeezed tightly to me. "You're sure you've never done this?"

"You haven't searched my name up?"

"You are extremely private."

"Meaning you thought I paid to keep quiet." I kissed her temple. "I didn't want the obligations of a relationship while I was solidifying my position."

Presley tensed and I saw why. Barika was standing with Marta on his arm a short distance away as if he was waiting for Presley to enter. Marta, while lovely, was no Presley. She was willowy, blonde, with fair, delicate features. In contrast, Barika was a lean, olive-skinned man, with black hair and rare blue eyes. Women flocked to him and his charisma, knowing he could help them break into showbusiness.

"I'm your real husband now. He can't touch you," I whispered, and she nodded distractedly.

"Gunner, how are you?" Melanie appeared on my left. I was so focused on Barika; I never saw her step up and kiss my cheek. She smiled knowingly at Presley and held out her hand with champagne in the other. "Melanie Kelley."

"Presley Laugesen." Presley was used to competitive women. She shook her hand before sliding comfortably back to my side.

Melanie unwittingly looked her up and down with her bright blue almond eyes. As usual, Melanie was stylish and perfectly manicured. Her raven locks were pinned with a diamond comb to her exposed shoulders.

"You look lovely, Penny." Presley went rigid on my arm.
It happened again. Barika snuck up on her right.
"I'm unsurprised to find you with child."
Melanie laughed.
I'd had just about enough.

CHAPTER 8
Presley

"Gunner Laugesen." He held his hand out to Barika. "Thank you."

Barika unknowingly shook his hand. Marta lifted hers.

Gunner smirked coolly at Barika. "For fucking up so I could marry my dream woman." He stared disdainfully at Marta's hand while my air caught painfully in my throat.

"You need bigger dreams." Barika laughed loudly. A sound I recognized as his obnoxious way of appearing more confident than he was.

Gunner stepped forward and the twit he'd been seeing gasped loudly, drawing attention. I was so sick of judging eyes on me. I dropped Gunner's arm and picked up my skirts. I cut to the side where I was hoping I could find a bathroom or a stairway.

There was both. The stairway led to the opulent bathroom where an attendant offered me a smile before I hurried into a stall. I put the seat down and covered my mouth.

There was no way I was going to go back out there and risk more altercations. Barika wouldn't leave. Gunner likely had a hundred more lovers hanging around. It had been a bad idea.

* * *

I waited hours before leaving the bathroom. My phone was shut off and I didn't know if Gunner waited around or if Torsten drove them back to Birdsong Estate.

Many of the people left. Other than the glances of recognition, some of disgust, a few of challenge, I was able to leave the building unscathed. I'd only bothered to look at their judgmental faces to see if Gunner was around.

The moment I reached the stairs I saw a blacked-out SUV's door opened. Gunner stepped out and didn't look my way. It wasn't a choice. I made him a deal. Other than the gratuitous sex, it was the most couple-like thing we'd done.

My eyes flitted to his hard face and he wouldn't look my way. I entered the SUV and the privacy panel was up. No smiles from Torsten. Gunner slammed the door after he sat.

It was a long, quiet drive home. If it was still my home.

Torsten must've been advised to stay in the car until we were inside. Olga wasn't at the door to greet us. Despite it being late, she never failed to meet me at the door with a beaming smile. I'd grown fond of the couple that never had any children. Gunner was their child.

We walked upstairs to our bedroom in silence and I wondered if we'd ever gone so long in one another's presence without saying a word.

I went directly into the bathroom and shut the door. My lower lip trembled as I faced my perfect face in the mirror. Most people would loathe me for being pretty and not happy enough. The door behind me opened and Gunner stepped inside.

"Where is your phone?" he demanded.

I pointed to the clutch on the counter.

Gunner eyed it.

"It's off."

Gunner nodded. "Where were you?"

"The bathroom," I answered.

I saw his throat work. "All night? Alone?"

"The bathroom attendant."

His brow drew down and he lifted his hard gaze to meet my eyes. "Is this funny to you?"

"No." My whisper was rough and soft.

"Stop joking." His nostrils flared and he turned around.

"I don't think I should go with to Denmark."

He stopped in his tracks. I watched him in the mirror. Instead of responding, he kept walking.

* * *

I couldn't sleep that night.

When I woke, Gunner was gone.

The tears came. I was too confused the night before to process my feelings and my first interaction with Barika after losing the trial had been jarring. Adding in all the other obstacles and I couldn't face it.

I forced myself from the bed and showered.

My phone was still off, so I powered it on and saw twenty-three missed texts from Gunner and forty voicemails. All from Gunner.

My heart twisted as I first read the texts. He was checking in to make sure I was okay. He apologized for losing his temper but promised that he walked away. Gunner said, he shouldn't have engaged, that *he* had *me* and that was why everyone was trying to come between us. They could see what we had was real. His final text asked asking me to meet him so we could dance, was to let me know that he understood he came on too strong and he'd leave me alone, but to please finish out the year.

I tortured myself with the voicemails. They started sweet and as he lost hope, turned solemn. Gunner wasn't angry, he was hurt.

I ran into the closet and grabbed an overnight bag from the center dresser's bottom drawer. I couldn't tell you what I threw inside. Packing was my only thought, not what to pack. I'd buy what I needed.

I raced down the stairs, holding my boots in my hand.

"Torsten!" I shouted.

"Presley? Are you hurt?" Olga called.

I wiped my cheeks. My hair was still wet and my clothes didn't match.

"Where in Denmark?"

Olga set her hands on my shoulders to calm me.

Impatience caused my heart to race. "Please, where did Gunner go? I met his ex and Barika was there with Marta. I was overwhelmed and I should've talked to him, but things became..." I inhaled shakily. "So much more than it was supposed to be and he scares me."

Olga cupped my face. "You love him."

I nodded and the tears came again. "I do and he is so upset with me."

She shook her head. "Did he tell you about his parents?"

I shook my head and she wiped my cheeks in a matronly way. "His father had a heart attack after catching his mother with another man. They were in the car together arguing and it crashed. Gunner is afraid of being hurt."

Impossibly, I felt worse.

"Oh no." I withdrew and covered my mouth. "I have to go to him. I think I hurt him."

Olga smiled fondly. "Torsten is by the pool."

I nodded. "Thank you, Olga." I kissed her cheek and took my things as I ran through the house.

Only, Torsten wasn't alone. Torsten looked from me to Gunner eating at the table overlooking the pull under an umbrella. Gunner's brow drew down so they were hidden behind his sunglasses. He wiped his mouth with the cloth napkin in his lap and stood as he set it aside.

I staggered forward.

Gunner wore a light sweater and pants for the cooling weather. He stopped before I could reach him.

"Good morning, Mrs. Laugesen."

"Good morning, Torsten," I breathed and kept walking to Gunner.

Gunner gave nothing away before I rushed him and slanted my mouth over his. He was rocked back and grabbed onto me.

"I thought you were leaving me," Gunner whispered.

I drew back and gaped at him. "Why would you think that?"

Gunner pushed his glasses into his hair. He looked to the bag I carried spilling clothes over the patio. I laughed and dropped it.

"I was going after you."

The corner of his mouth kicked up. "Really?"

I nodded. "I should've talked to you about it last night. It all came rushing back. I... I don't want to lose you."

CHAPTER 9

Gunner

I sighed and her smile fell.

She reversed from me and I frowned. "That sigh —"

"Are you enjoying yourself here?" I asked her and she narrowed her eyes. She hadn't looked at me that way since the first week she arrived.

"Just get to the point. Are you saying I should take this bag and go?" Her voice took on a coolness I'd never heard from her.

"I'm saying... forever."

Presley's expression smoothed. Her lips began to curl. "I love you, Gunner."

I bit my lower lip as I smiled at her and she leaned forward to wrap her arms around my neck. I ran my hands along her arms to her ribs and sighed again.

"I fell in love with you while watching you play Swan."

She laughed and leaned on her tiptoes to kiss me. "Finally the truth. I already knew. This, *us*, has a much better end."

Afterword

For more from Charli Rahe, please visit www.charlirahe.com and join Charli's Devils on Facebook.

Her novels can be found at most major book retailers and Kindle Unlimited.

Made in the USA
Monee, IL
12 June 2025